The Contest

The Contest

ADAPTED AND ILLUSTRATED

BY NONNY HOGROGIAN

GREENWILLOW BOOKS

A DIVISION OF WILLIAM MORROW & CO., INC., NEW YORK

*An Armenian
Pronunciation Guide*

THE PLACE
Erzingah: *Air* zing ah

THE CHARACTERS
Ehleezah: *Eh* leez ah
Hmayag: *Huh* my ag
Hrahad: *Huh* rah had
The Ishkhan: *Ish* khan

Library of Congress Cataloging in Publication Data   Hogrogian, Nonny. The contest.
Summary: An Armenian folktale about two robbers courting the same girl.   [1. Folklore — Armenia]   I.
Title   PZ8.1.H723Co4   398.2'2'095662   75-40389   ISBN 0-688-80042-4   ISBN 0-688-84042-6 lib. bdg.

For David

 High in the mountains, near the village of Erzingah, there lived two robbers named Hmayag and Hrahad.

Hmayag did his robbing by day and spent his evenings with Ehleezah, his betrothed.

Hrahad did his robbing at night and spent his days with his future wife, whose name, too, was Ehleezah.

The truth of the matter is they were both betrothed to the same Ehleezah although they didn't know each other.

One evening while Hmayag was visiting Ehleezah and Hrahad was out looking for riches for her, each of the robbers thought about his future. Each decided it was time to try his luck in the next province. The men made their preparations and Ehleezah gave each of them a bokhjah of food for the journey.

Hmayag left early in the morning as usual, since he liked to work by day. Minutes later Hrahad departed, to be sure he would reach his destination by nightfall.

As it turned out, the two robbers met at noon under a pomegranate tree where each of them had stopped for lunch. They introduced themselves and opened their bokhjahs to see what Ehleezah had packed for them.

Hmayag pulled out some cheese and olives, and so did Hrahad. Hrahad pulled out a small jar of dried meat. So did Hmayag. In addition, each bokhjah contained one tomato, three scallions, and four large apricots.

The robbers were amazed at the coincidence, and they sensed a strong common bond. They continued the trip together and compared their lives.

"I earn my living by my cleverness," said Hmayag.

"So do I."

"I will confess to you that I am a robber," said Hmayag.

"So am I."

"I live on the hill above the village of Erzingah," said Hmayag.

"So do I."

"And I am betrothed to Ehleezah, the sweetest girl in our mountains."

"So am I."

"No, I am," insisted Hmayag.

The two men grew excited and each described his girl. Before long, they discovered the truth.

"I cannot say that I am happy about your pilfering my mountains," said Hmayag, "but you certainly cannot marry my future wife!"

"But she's mine!" shouted Hrahad, and the argument continued this way and that until the two robbers realized that anger would not settle their problem.

"Well, since our sweet deceiver must give up one of us, let us decide which one it will be," agreed Hmayag and Hrahad, each with great confidence in himself. They decided to have a contest to see which of them was the cleverest thief in these mountains. The winner would marry Ehleezah.

Since there was still some daylight when they entered the walls of the city, Hmayag took his turn first. They noticed a man with a small bundle walking toward the jewelry shop. Hmayag quietly slipped the bundle away from the man, and when he saw it contained jewels, he quickly replaced them with stones and returned the bundle to the man.

Needless to say, both the man and the jeweler were a little surprised when the bundle was opened. The man reddened, muttered a few words, picked up the package, and left.

While the man hurried home, Hmayag again slipped the bundle away from him, replaced the jewels, and returned the bundle. The two smiling robbers followed the man to see the results of their trickery. The man's wife listened to his torrent of anger while the robbers watched through the window. She opened the bundle and found the jewels.

"What are you talking about?" she asked. "Why would I give you stones instead of jewels?"

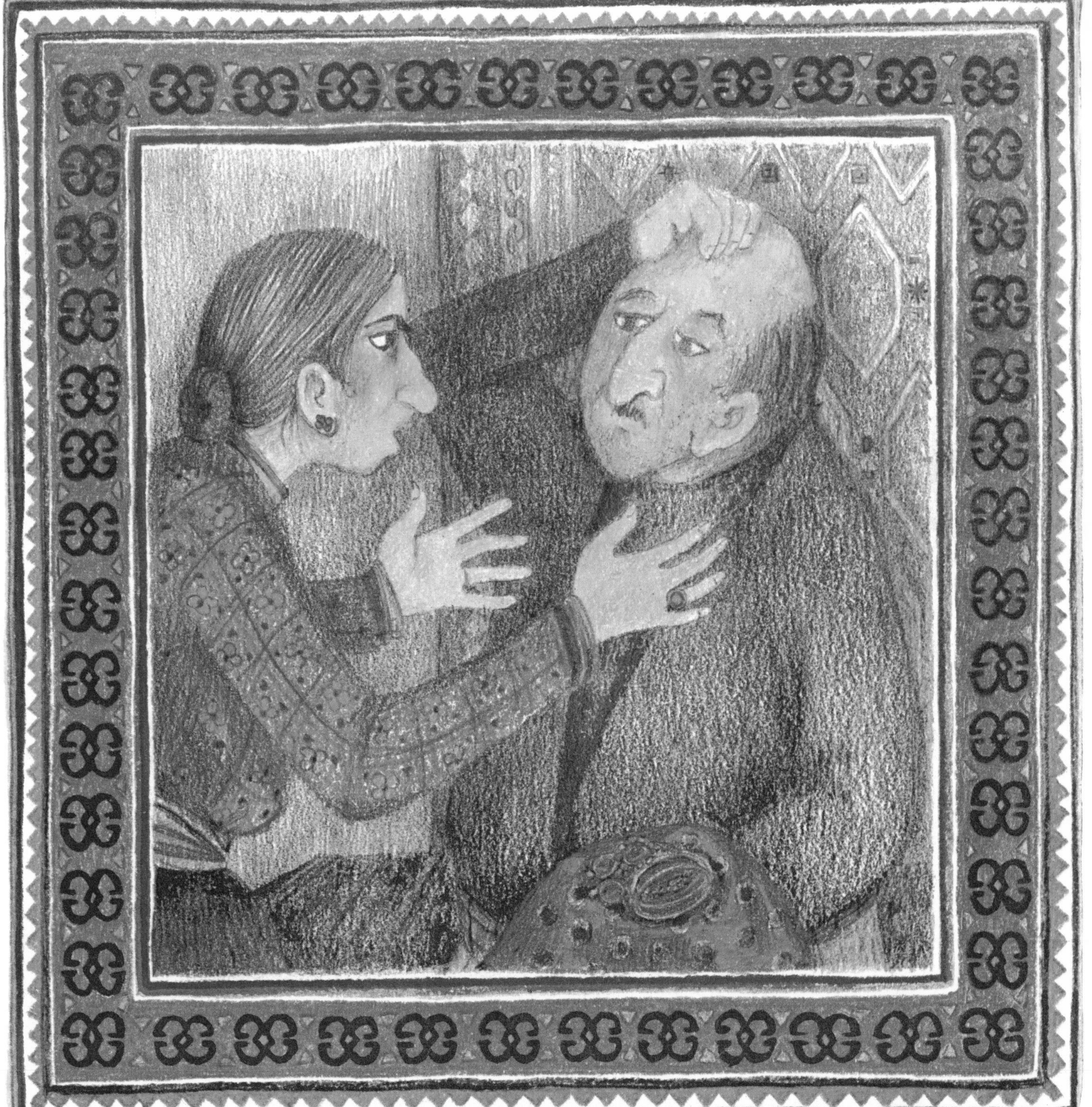

The confused man tied the bundle and started out again for the jewelry shop. But Hmayag hadn't finished with him yet. Once more he slipped the jewels out of the bundle and slipped the stones in, and the two robbers trailed the man to see what would happen. And once again the poor man was shocked when the bundle was opened. The jeweler was beginning to lose his patience. The man gathered the bundle of stones and ran from the store.

The robbers were doubled over with laughter, but Hmayag pulled himself up and continued the game. The jewels once more replaced the stones, and it did no good for the man to yell at his wife when he arrived home because she proved again that he was acting like a fool.

"Have your eyes gotten weak or is it your mind?" she shouted. "Now take my jewels and have them repaired before something really happens to them."

So the man started out for the third time, and for the third time
Hmayag substituted the stones for the jewels. The man arrived at
the shop and the jeweler opened the bundle and found the stones.
He was certain the man was playing a joke on him and he threw
him out of his store.

"Don't ever come back!" he shouted.

In the end, of course, there was no need to go back since Hmayag
kept the jewels.

"Now since night is beginning to fall," Hmayag said to his companion, "let me see how clever you are."

Hrahad found some spikes and a hammer and led Hmayag to the Ishkhan's palace. He told Hmayag to sit on his shoulders, and they climbed the palace wall, hammering in the spikes as they went.

Once inside the wall, Hmayag remembered that he was getting hungry.

"Well, then," said Hrahad, "we shall have a feast."

He took the plumpest hen from the Ishkhan's henhouse, lit a fire, and roasted their dinner. Hmayag was a little concerned that the fire might be noticed, but there were no guards in sight, and when the meal was done, they left the bones.

They entered the palace, and Hrahad went straight to the Ishkhan's quarters with Hmayag following carefully. There was a sleepy guard outside the door who was chewing on pinesap to keep himself awake. Hrahad threw a pebble against the wall. The noise surprised the guard and he dropped the pinesap. After he checked the hall and was convinced the noise was his imagination, he went back to his post, but the pinesap was gone. Five minutes later the guard was asleep.

The robbers entered the Ishkhan's room. Hrahad shook the bed and aroused him. In his state of half-sleep the Ishkhan asked what had happened, and Hrahad told him that he was needed to make an important decision.

"Once upon a time," Hrahad said, "there were two robbers who were betrothed to the same woman."

"How could that be?" mumbled the sleepy Ishkhan.

"The robbers didn't know it," said Hrahad, "until one day they both decided to go to the same neighboring province."

Hrahad described the day's events. He told the Ishkhan how they discovered Ehleezah's secret and how they set up a contest to see which robber would have her for his wife.

The Ishkhan thought he was having an amusing dream.

Hrahad told him in detail about the day-robber who stole the same jewels from the same man three times, and the Ishkhan agreed that this was indeed a very clever robber.

Then Hrahad told him how the night-robber got them over the palace wall and stole a hen from the palace henhouse and built a fire and roasted the hen, and how they ate the hen and left the bones behind. In addition the robbers had had the audacity to enter the Ishkhan's quarters.

"Impossible," said the smiling Ishkhan. "They would have been caught coming over the wall or certainly before they had finished eating the hen. The story can't be true."

"Perhaps not," said Hrahad, "but tell me, wise Ishkhan, if the story were true, which one would you pick as the cleverer of the two?"

"Oh, without question I would choose the night-robber," said the Ishkhan. "But on the other hand, the day-robber was very clever too." With that he turned over to dream another dream.

The next morning the Ishkhan awoke remembering a dream about two clever robbers. And the Ishkhan's guards agreed it would be better not to tell the Ishkhan about the chicken bones they had found near the palace door. In the meantime Hrahad and Hmayag decided their sweet betrayer didn't deserve either of them. They agreed that this province could provide a profitable future for both of them and they remained there.

And back in Erzingah Ehleezah, too, had discovered a new future.